Adapted from the film
by Justine Korman and Ron Fontes

New York

Printed in the United States of America.

First Edition
1 3 5 7 9 10 8 6 4 2

This book is set in 14-point Hiroshige Book.

Library of Congress Catalog Card Number: 98-85036
ISBN: 0-7868-4252-0 (paperback)

For more Disney Press fun visit www.DisneyBooks.com

Chapter 1

Princess Atta looked up to the sky. "Wind's died down. They'll be here soon. I mean, we're on schedule, right? We should have a total by now." The young ant was nervous. This was Atta's first time in charge of the annual Ant Island harvest. Soon she would take over from her mother, the Queen.

She turned to Thorny, head of the colony's Engineering Department. The council member rapidly rattled beads on his ant abacus. "I'm still counting, Princess."

"Right, right, right." Atta tapped her foot impatiently. She spread her shiny wings to hover over Thorny's shoulder.

"Your highness, I can't count when you hover like that," Thorny said. His fingers shook as he slid more beads in the frame.

Atta sighed and landed. "Right. Sorry, sorry."

Atta would soon be responsible for everything she could see. The anthill was a cone enclosing the long, twisted root of a tall tree. The gnarled root arched over a small clearing at the base of the tree. Where its branches forked, the tree bore a single knothole.

The ants used the tree as a calendar. In winter, the tree was bare. Buds meant spring. Green leaves shaded their home in the summer. When those leaves turned to gold and fell, the ants harvested.

Worker ants streamed up a ramp to a big, flat rock called the offering stone. Cornelius, head of the Agriculture Department, was last in line.

Mr. Soil of the colony's Education Department, Dr. Flora of Health and Ant Services, and Atta's mother, the colony's queen, gathered around the princess. The dignified old queen adjusted her crown, then stroked her pet aphid.

"How's my beautiful daughter doing on her first official job?" the Queen asked over Aphie's yips.

Atta sighed. "Mother, I don't think I'm cut out for this. What if something goes wrong?"

"It'll be fine," her mother assured her. "It's the same year after year: They come, they eat, they leave. That's our lot in life. It's not a lot, but it's our life." The Queen chuckled at her own joke. "You don't become queen overnight, Atta. That's why you're in training."

Suddenly, dirt squirted up and two little ant boys popped out of the ground. Right behind them was a tiny girl ant.

"Hey, come back here!" the girl shouted at the boys. Her tiny wings fluttered in a futile attempt to fly and she fell flat on her face.

The Queen was stern. "Dot!"

Princess Atta's little sister slowly turned around. Dot was caked with dirt, but her voice was that of an angel. "Yes, Mother?"

"What did I tell you about trying to fly?" the Queen demanded. Aphie squirmed in her arms.

"Not until my wings grow in," Dot repeated dutifully. She was sick of hearing this.

Atta said, "Dot, you're still too little to play with those other kids. You should just—"

"Excuse me," Dot interrupted in a regal tone. After all, she was a princess, too. "I was talking to Mother. You're not the queen yet, Atta."

"Be nice to your sister," said the Queen, struggling to control the wriggly aphid.

"It's not my fault she's so stressed out!" Dot argued.

"I'm not stressed out!" Atta yelled.

Just then a huge wheat stalk toppled right on top of Princess Atta. The royal ant vanished beneath kernels of golden grain.

The Ant Council was shocked! A second stalk flopped just inches away. Was the world coming to an end? Had THEY arrived early? What could wreak such awful destruction?

"It's Flik!" Thorny shouted. The ant colony had its own walking disaster area. How one little worker could spread such havoc was more than any ant could imagine. Their whole society was based on tradition. Things were done the way they had always been done. New ideas were viewed with suspicion. In their orderly world, Flik was a freak!

Flik was a little bug with big ideas. His small, round head swarmed with dreams of great things! New inventions! Patented methods! Improvements! Tools! Efficiency! The colony could be so much better, if only they would give Flik a chance.

Actually, the colony had endured several of Flik's inventions. They were still fixing many of his "improvements." Flik knew that someday one of his ideas would work. It had to! And then all the other ants would stop laughing at him. And maybe, just maybe, they would respect him because he was different, not hate him for it. Until then, he would just keep having new ideas.

Flik's latest invention was a machine to harvest grain in half the time it normally took. His mechanized harvester was a gangly assembly of twigs and reeds strapped to his glossy thorax. Its whirring buzz saw blade chopped wheat stalks, and a spring-loaded trough shook the grain into a leaf basket. Then the stalk was ejected by the spring. Unfortunately, Princess Atta was in the line of fire.

The council scolded Flik. "What do you think you're doing?" Thorny thundered. "You could have killed somebody!"

Flik lifted his protective bark visor (another patented Flik invention). "I'm sorry! Please forgive me!" Then Flik recognized Atta's curly antennae poking up through the grain. "Oh, no!" he gasped. Flik loved the princess from afar, when he wasn't busy building something.

Quickly, Flik and the others lifted the wheat stalk off the fallen princess. Atta coughed and sputtered as she dusted herself off. "Flik, what are you doing?"

"Huh?" Flik blushed whenever the princess was near. "Oh, this is my new idea for harvesting grain," he bubbled. "No more picking individual kernels. You just cut down the entire stalk!"

Atta was exasperated. "I appreciate your enthusiasm, but—"

"I thought of something else," Flik said breathlessly. "You're gonna love this!" He picked an ordinary blade of grass and a bead of dew. Flik rolled the grass into a cone, which held the sparkling dewdrop. "A telescope!" he announced with a flourish.

Dot giggled. The Queen laughed. Flik gazed at Atta through his telescope. She was even more beautiful!

The Ant Council was not impressed. To tell the truth, the Council disapproved of the troublemaker's antics. Flik was crazy!

"The princess doesn't have time for this," Thorny declared. "She should be addressing more important matters. We've got to get the offering stone filled up, or we are in big, big trouble."

"Big, big trouble," Cornelius echoed.

Atta couldn't help liking Flik, but she wished the nutty ant could control himself. "Please, Flik, just get in line and pick grain like everybody else," she said politely.

"I'm sorry," Flik stammered. "I was really just trying to . . . "

Instead of an answer, Cornelius merely pointed to the field.

Flik shuffled sadly toward the wheat field. He was used to rejection, but that didn't make it hurt any less. The council watched while the inventor disappeared among the stalks of wheat.

Cornelius sniffed. "Harvester! Why, we've harvested the same way since I was a pupa."

Princess Dot picked up the dew telescope. While the grown-ups rambled on, Dot ran into the field after Flik. "Hey, Flik! Wait up!" she cried.

"Oh, hello, Princess," Flik said.

"You can call me Dot," she offered. "You forgot this." She held up the telescope. Flik wasn't like the other grown-ups. He still knew how to play. Flik's inventions were the coolest toys, even when they didn't work!

"Thanks," said Flik. "You keep it. I can make another."

Princess Dot smiled. "I like your inventions."

"Really? Well, you're the first. I'm beginning to think that nothing I do works," Flik said sadly.

The princess peered through the rolled grass blade. "This works!"

"Great, one success. I'm never going to make a difference," Flik moaned.

"Me, neither," Dot agreed. "Everyone says I'm too little."

"Being little isn't such a bad thing," Flik replied.

"Is, too."

"Is not."

A rapid exchange of many *is not*s and *is, too*s followed. How could he explain this to a kid? "I need a seed," Flik said suddenly. He grunted and strained, but couldn't reach around his back to take a wheat kernel out of his basket. Hmm . . . a flaw in the design. He'd have to work on that. Meanwhile, the clever ant picked up a pebble from the sandy soil. "Pretend that's a seed," he said.

"It's a rock," Dot observed realistically, like a proper ant.

"Use your imagination! We'll pretend it's a seed. Do you see that tree?" Flik asked. "Everything that made that giant tree is already inside this tiny little seed. Some time, a little bit of sunshine and rain . . . you have a tree!"

11

Dot was skeptical. "This rock will be a tree?"

"Imagination! A *seed* will be a tree. You might not feel like you can do much now, but that's because you're not a tree yet. You have to give yourself time. You're still a seed," Flik explained.

"But it's a rock!" Dot insisted.

Flik flailed the arms of his mechanical grain picker in frustration. "Yes, it's a rock! I know a rock when I see one. I've spent a lot of time around rocks."

Princess Dot giggled. "You're weird. I like you!"

Just then the colony alarm sounded. Flik looked to the sky. "They're here!"

Chapter 2

Orderly lines of ants dissolved into a mass of screaming, frantic bugs, all antennae and elbows. Atta tried to get everyone calmly into the anthill, but no one would listen to her.

Princess Dot emerged from the wheat field and ran to her mother. Relieved that her youngest daughter was safe, the Queen whistled loudly. The crowd stopped in its tracks. The Queen announced, "Okay, everyone! Single file. Food to the offering stone and everyone into the anthill. Let's go!"

As if by magic, order was restored. The colony funneled into the sandy cone of the anthill. Thousands of workers marched down the spiral root that was the hill's center support. Soon the ants were safe in a huge, underground bunker lit by glowing greenish mushrooms. The Queen sat on her throne with the council and her beloved Princess Dot at her side.

Atta waited outside for stragglers. When the last ant disappeared from view, the princess flew into the hill.

But one ant was A.W.O.L. Flik's harvester had become tangled in the wheat stalks out in the field.

"Hey, wait for me!" Flik called. The harvester was hopelessly jammed! Flik scrambled out of the awkward harness. He dropped the harvester beside the offering stone while he ran to safety.

Unfortunately, Flik had forgotten to turn his invention off. A spring went *SPROING!* and knocked a leg out from under the offering stone. The big, flat rock tilted. As Flik watched in horror, all the food tumbled off the stone into a puddle in the riverbed below Ant Island. Flik tried to stop the disaster, but he was too late. One puny ant could not right the massive rock.

"Oh, no!" Flik moaned as the last grain tumbled into oblivion. He could already hear an eerie buzzing in the sky. THEY were coming! Flik panicked. He ran to the bunker crying, "Princess Atta! Princess Atta!"

Flik pushed past hundreds of ants huddled in terror. Finally, he reached the princess. "There's something I need to tell you!" Flik gasped. The colony was doomed!

"Not now," Atta said, listening to the ominous drone above.

"Your Highness, it's about the offering." The princess shushed the inventor as the buzzing grew louder and louder. Suddenly, the sound stopped. The ants heard footsteps on the earth above them. Then a loud voice said, "Hey, what's goin' on?"

A second voice said, "Yeah. Where's the food?"

The whole colony gasped in horror. Atta suddenly realized something. She looked at Flik and calmly asked, "What did you do?"

The entire colony looked at Flik.

"It was an accident," he mumbled.

A huge, jointed foot burst through the ceiling and a shaft of sunlight pierced the gloom.

The colony screamed as more giant feet punched down into the bunker.

Grasshoppers jumped through the holes. Ants ran in every direction. The gang of huge grasshoppers picked up handfuls of ants, searching for food.

Three grasshoppers tossed Flik back and forth like a ball. When the green giants lost interest in this sport, they dropped him. Flik tried to crawl to safety, only to find himself at the feet of the biggest grasshopper, a towering terror of plated armor with four jointed arms and long, spiked legs. A pair of wings hung like a cape off his strong shoulders. The leader's right eye was a cloudy gray and his good left eye blazed bright yellow.

"H-H-Hopper!" Flik stammered. Hopper was a name used to frighten naughty pupae in the ant nursery.

The grasshopper stepped over Flik and strode casually through the colony. The crowd parted wherever Hopper strutted. He looked around the bunker, and with his back to the colony, said calmly, "So, where is it?"

The ants didn't know what to say.

Hopper turned and bellowed, "WHERE'S MY FOOD?"

The ants flinched.

"Isn't it up there?" Atta asked meekly.

Hopper studied the princess. He put a hand to his antennae, as if he were hard of hearing. "What? Excuse me?"

Atta nervously said, "The food was in a leaf sitting on top of . . . are you sure it's not up there?"

"Are you saying I'm stupid?" Hopper demanded. "Let's think about the logic, shall we? If the food was up there, would I come down to your level looking for it? Why am I even talking to you? You don't smell like the Queen."

"She's learning to take over for me," the Queen said with immense dignity.

"I see. Under new management. So it's *your* fault." Hopper glared at Princess Atta.

Atta pointed to the very guilty-looking Flik. "No, it was—"

Hopper cut her off. "Ah, ah. First rule of

leadership: Everything is your fault." Hopper picked up the princess and set her down beside him. "Come here. Let Uncle Hopper teach you how things are supposed to work. You see, Nature has a certain order. The sun grows the food, the ants pick the food, the grasshoppers eat the food."

"And the birds eat the grasshoppers," Hopper's brother, Molt, interjected. "Hey, like the one that nearly ate you, remember?" Molt scratched at his perpetually peeling armor. "You should've seen it. This blue jay had Hopper halfway down his throat, and Hopper's kickin' and screamin', okay?"

Hopper glared at his brother and said sternly, "Molt!"

"Come on, Hopper. It's a great story," Molt said.

The leader grabbed Molt's raggedy antennae and dragged him to the back wall of the bunker. "If I hadn't promised Mom I wouldn't kill you, I'd kill you!" The furious Hopper cocked his fist, ready to punch his brother.

Molt squealed, "Remember Ma!"

The frustrated gang leader punched another grasshopper, then turned to look at the horrified ants. "I'm a compassionate insect," Hopper explained. "In fact, I'm willing to forget this whole no-food thing."

A wave of relief swept over the colony.

Then Hopper continued, "On the other hand, there are still a few months till the rains come. So you can all try again."

The Queen objected. "Hopper, we need that time to gather food for ourselves."

"You should have thought of that before you put *her* in charge." The gang leader pointed at Princess Atta. "Now listen, if you can't keep your end of the bargain, I can't guarantee your safety. There are insects out there that would take advantage of you. Someone could get hurt."

A horrible cackle echoed in the cavern. Two gang members held the straining chain of a monster grasshopper who slavered and growled. Dot panicked and turned to run, bumping into Hopper's leg. He picked her up and dangled her near the monster.

"You don't like Thumper?" Hopper asked with a cruel laugh.

The tiny but brave princess did not cry, though she hung just inches from the creature's dripping jaws.

Flik could stand no more. He stepped forward. "Leave her alone!" The little ant froze when he realized what he'd done.

Hopper swung Dot over Flik's head. "You want her? Go ahead, take her!"

Flik's courage evaporated like a dewdrop in the sun. The big grasshopper was twice Flik's size, had twice as many arms, and ten times the meanness. Ashamed at his helplessness, Flik just looked at his feet.

Hopper sneered. "No? Then get back in line." He dropped Dot. The little princess ran into her mother's arms. Hopper surveyed the scene. "It seems to me that you ants are forgetting your place, so let's double the order of food."

The ants were too afraid even to gasp. Only Atta spoke up. "No!"

Hopper silenced Atta with a glance from his

good eye. "It's a bug-eat-bug world out there, my little friends." The gang leader stalked across the chamber to join his hench-hoppers. He paused by Molt and peeled a sheet of skin off his brother's flaky shoulder. He held the filmy sheet of chiton in a shaft of sunlight.

"We'll be back at the end of the season, when the last leaf falls." The skin fluttered gracefully to the ground like an autumn leaf. "You ants have a nice summer," Hopper told the colony. To his gang, he shouted, "Let's ride!"

The chamber was filled with the whirr of glistening grasshopper wings. The whole world seemed to buzz as the greedy gang shot up into the blue sky.

Chapter 3

A judge's gavel banged on a small rock as the Ant Council met in the colony courtroom. The council had been discussing the current crisis. The proceedings grew a bit frantic, so Atta called for order. "Please read back the charges."

Dr. Flora shuffled a stack of leaves. She had made notes during the long meeting. "Oh, my. Well, we talked about more food for Hopper . . . less food for ourselves . . . possible starvation . . . and then there was all that yelling. Oh, golly, give me a minute here."

"Just the highlights, please," Atta said wearily.

The elderly queen nodded off in her throne while Aphie snored in her arms. Someone tapped a pencil. Another Council member drummed his digits on a polished rock. Dr.

Flora cleared her throat. "We're doomed, and it's all Flik's fault."

Despite the fact that she liked Flik, Atta obviously agreed. The princess regarded the miserable inventor. "What do you have to say for yourself?"

"I'm sorry for the way I am. I just had an idea to speed up production . . . " Flik felt flat. An accident had squished his dreams.

Cornelius harumphed. "I've survived eighty seasons without a new idea." His stare dared anyone in the room to challenge his wisdom.

"I didn't want things to go wrong," Flik explained. "I especially didn't want you to look bad, Princess. I was just trying to help."

"Then help us by not helping us!" Mr. Soil said coldly.

"*Help*," Flik muttered. An idea sprouted. And while it grew in his brain, Flik ignored the council's windy discussion.

Atta had reached a decision. "Flik, you are sentenced to one month digging in the tunnels."

"Excuse me, Your Highness," Thorny

protested. "Need I remind you of Flik's tunnel-within-a-tunnel project? The Engineering Department spent two days digging him out. Send him to Health and Ant Services."

Dr. Flora cried, "Heavens, no! Let Agriculture have him."

"He just came from the Agriculture Department. That's why we're in this mess," Cornelius blustered. "Give him to Education."

Mr. Soil was disgusted. "Oh, fine, dump him in my lap. Like we don't have enough children already."

"It's perfect!" Flik cried with sudden enthusiasm.

The argument stopped. Flik had the Queen's attention. "Perfect? What's perfect?" she asked.

Flik said, "Your Highness, we could send someone to get help!"

The Council had never heard such an outrageous idea.

"Leave the island?" Atta asked. Such un-antly behavior was inconceivable! The whole idea was . . . repugnant!

"Why didn't I think of that?" the Queen wondered. "Oh, because it's suicide!"

"She's right! We never leave the island," Thorny added.

"Never leave!" Cornelius echoed.

Thorny knew many reasons why not to leave Ant Island. The Council member ticked them off on his mental abacus, "There's snakes and birds and bigger bugs out there!"

"Exactly!" Flik exclaimed. "We could find bigger bugs to come here and fight and rid us of Hopper and his gang forever!"

Mr. Soil shook his antennae. "Ludicrous!"

"Who would do a crazy thing like that?" Dr. Flora wondered.

"I would!" Flik volunteered.

The Queen laughed. "You've got a lot of spunk, kid. But no one's gonna help a bunch of ants."

"At least we could try," Flik argued. "I could travel to the city!"

"Your search would take weeks," Atta pointed out.

The Council's antennae perked up. Weeks?

Something that would keep the jinx out of the colony for weeks?

"Royal huddle!" Thorny cried, and the members clustered around the queen-to-be. "It's perfect!" Thorny declared.

Atta was confused. "What's perfect?"

"We'll let Flik leave . . . " Mr. Soil began, " . . . while we keep harvesting to meet Hopper's demand," Cornelius concluded.

"With Flik gone," Dr. Flora said, "He can't . . . "

" . . . mess anything up!" Princess Atta finally saw the light at the top of the anthill. With Flik gone, nothing could go wrong. The colony might actually survive her first harvest as queen!

Flik was surprised when Atta announced that she had decided to grant his request. "Thank you for this chance! I promise I won't mess up!" Flik gushed. "But shouldn't I help repair some of the damage before I go?"

"No!" Atta cried hastily. "Just go! Go!"

The Council joined her. "Go! Go!"

Dawn found the colony busily rebuilding

the offering stone and patching the slope of the anthill. Dressed like a jungle commando and clanking with gear, Flik marched through the arch of the root. He waved to the busy workers. "Don't worry! The colony is in good hands," he said as he passed under the gnarled gateway.

A huge cheer roared behind Flik. His chest puffed with pride. The distracted inventor thought the colony was applauding him. Flik was lucky he didn't realize they were merely glad to see him go.

Two ant boys ran up to the deluded hero. "My dad says you'll come crying back to the colony in an hour," one told Flik.

The other shook his antennae. "My dad's betting you're going to die. He says if the heat doesn't get you, the birds will."

Flik swallowed hard. Then a little voice piped up. "I think he's gonna make it." Flik looked down and saw Dot scrambling up the boulder behind them. "You watch. He's going to get the biggest, roughest bugs you've ever seen!"

"Nobody asked you, Your Royal Shortness," the first boy teased.

"Yeah, Dot. What do you know?" the other demanded.

"Ease up," Flik protested. "She's entitled to her opinion."

By then Flik and the kids had reached the top of the big boulder that bordered the colony. The wide world stretched out below them. Flik jumped off the edge to a fuzzy dandelion puff. He pulled out a fluffy seed. The curious children watched.

Flik took a deep breath and said, "Here I go! For the colony! And for oppressed ants everywhere!" Flik held the fluff to the wind. His feet left the ground. "Whoa . . . " Flik felt dizzy. Workers weren't supposed to fly.

"Wow!" Dot exclaimed as Flik floated higher, up and away from Ant Island. Dot couldn't wait to fly, but her wings just weren't big enough yet.

The boys were impressed—until Flik crashed in the dry riverbed. Dot gasped in alarm, but her hero quickly pulled himself back onto his feet. "I'm . . . okay," Flik called.

The ant boy told his friend, "Your dad's right. He's gonna die."

Princess Dot wasn't listening. "Good luck, Flik!" she shouted.

With a final wave, Flik was gone!

Chapter 4

"Back! Get back, you horrible beast! Hai-yah!" Rosie the spider cracked a shoelace like a whip.

A ferocious-looking rhino beetle reared up and roared on top of a gleaming thimble. Spotlights sparkled on the huge bug's enormous horn and glossy dark shell. He was a fearsome sight, and the flies in the stands were suitably impressed. Seeing a monster like this was the reason they came to the circus—that and the stale popcorn.

Then the shoelace snapped against one of the big beetle's feet. The roar choked in his throat, and the beetle sobbed like a baby. He fell over on his back and feebly wiggled his wounded tootsy. The circus band's rousing music ground to a sour stop.

"Oh, my goodness!" Rosie rushed to fix the

boo-boo."I'm sorry, Dim. Show Rosie the owie," the spider cooed.

"Boooooo! Boo!" The few flies occupying the nearly empty bleachers under P. T. Flea's big top were not happy. One mother fly even said, "I've been in outhouses that didn't stink this bad."

While Rosie comforted the sobbing beetle, many members of the audience left the tent. "I want my money back!" an irate fly yelled.

"No refunds after the first two minutes," P. T. Flea sputtered. The portly flea wore a faded, fancy suit and a shiny top hat. P. T. had been in showbiz all his life and was actually more of a humbug than a flea. When the customers wanted their money back, P. T. knew it was time to flee.

P. T. leaped to the backstage entrance and poked his tiny top hat through the tissue curtain. The agitated circus owner addressed a trio of clowns. A caterpillar, a ladybug, and a walking stick climbed into their costumes in the crowded Clown Alley. "We're losing the audience! You bozos get out there!" P. T. shouted.

"I hate performing on an empty stomach," the chubby caterpillar complained.

"Do your act, Heimlich, then you can eat," P. T. promised the blubbery clown. The constantly consuming caterpillar was eating P. T. out of doghouse and tent!

"What's the point of going out there? They'll only laugh at me," the fussy walking stick griped bitterly.

"That's because you're a *clown*, Slim," P. T. replied. He wondered why clowns were always so grumpy.

Slim threw his usual fit. "No, it's because I'm a *prop*! You always cast me as a broom, a pole, a splinter—"

"You're a walking stick. It's funny. Now go!" P. T. commanded.

Slim angrily strapped a flower to his head. The round red ladybug beside him daintily adjusted a similar flower. Slim stalked through the curtain past P. T. "Parasite," he sniffed.

As the "flowers" entered the ring, the cricket band struck up a lively tune. The sleepy fireflies in the rigging shone their spotlights on

"They're here!" Flik yells, looking to the sky.

The ant colony races to safety inside the anthill bunker.

"Where's the food?" Hopper bellows at the frightened ants.

"So it's your fault the food is missing," Hopper accuses Atta.

"Leave Dot alone!" Flik yells at Hopper.

"Tra, la, la, spring is in the air," Slim recites in his flower costume.

"Ooh! Candy corn! Let me help you finish it!" Heimlich offers.

"So bein' a ladybug makes me a GIRL, is that it, flyboy?" Francis yells at the flies.

"Flaming Death!" P. T. Flea exclaims.

Flik has finally done something right—he returns with warriors to fight off the grasshoppers.

"This meeting's classified," Flik tells Atta—he can't let her learn the truth about the circus bugs.

"You can't go!" Flik tells the circus bugs after they find out he wants them to fight the grasshoppers.

Flik gives Atta a big thumbs-up.

"Sorry, no one's seen any circus performers around here," Flik declares, trying to hide the circus poster.

"Ta-daa!" Tuck and Roll are able to distract Hopper and his gang by making them laugh.

Manny and Gypsy perfom the ultimate magic act—making the Queen disappear!

the reluctant performers. Slim said, "Tra, la, la, la. Spring is in the air. And I am a flower with nothing interesting to say."

The ladybug looked offstage, with a bored imitation of surprise.

"A bee!" Slim said.

Heimlich inched out in his snug, crude bee costume. "I am a cute little bumblebee. Here I come to nestle in your petals and taste your sweet nectar," the caterpillar recited as his sluggish segments oozed past the stands. Heimlich's stomach grumbled when he noticed a little fly eating candy. "Ooh! Candy corn!" Heimlich exclaimed. "Let me help you finish it."

Meanwhile, two flies were heckling the ladybug. "Hey, cutie! You want to pollinate with a real bug?" one bellowed.

"Ooh, yeah! Come to papa!" the other leered.

The ladybug approached the hecklers with a demure smile, then leaned in. "So bein' a ladybug automatically makes me a GIRL? Is that it, flyboy?" he shouted in a drill sergeant's bray.

The flies were shocked. "She's a guy!"

"Francis, leave the flies alone," Heimlich urged. "They have poo-poo hands."

But the macho ladybug was out of control. This was a sore point with Francis. He hated it when people mistook him for a lady.

P. T. slapped his forehead. "Not again!" The owner bounced backstage while Francis roared, "Judging by your breath, you must have been buzzing around a dung heap all day!"

Slim and Heimlich struggled to pull Francis back into the ring. "Come on, Francis, you're making the maggots cry," Slim said.

Backstage, P. T. hustled the next act. "All right! We're dyin' out there! Gypsy, quick! You and Manny—"

"OOOOOoooommmmmm." Manny the Magnificent, the proud praying mantis magician, chanted in lotus position. His lovely moth assistant, Gypsy, applied makeup before a mirror. Her huge wings, when folded, looked harmless. But when unfurled, they flashed a fierce face. The pale, pretty moth whispered, "Shh! He's in a trance."

"Well, get him out of it!" P. T. yelled. "You and your husband are up NOW!"

With immense dignity, the mantis rose from his seat. "Yet again, it is up to me to rescue the performance. Gypsy, come!" Manny collided with some scenery.

"The other way, Manny, dear," Gypsy said gently. Manny may have been a great magician, but he was a tad absentminded.

"Yes, of course," Manny responded as if nothing had happened.

Under the big top, Francis and the flies were still locked in combat. "Any time, pal!" the ladybug screeched. "I'm gonna pick the hairs out of your head one by one!"

"Take your best shot!" the fly taunted, as Slim and Heimlich dragged the furious ladybug to safety. Francis punched the air with all four fists.

"Let me handle this," Slim whispered. He turned to the flies. "That's no way to speak to a lady," Slim chided.

"I heard that, you twig!" Francis fumed.

Just then, P. T. jumped onto the center stage

thimble. "Ladies and gentlebugs! Allow me to present Manto the Magnificent and his lovely assistant, Gypsy!"

The flea struck a penny gong. The fireflies shined their lights through a red lollipop to cast an eerie glow upon the magician.

Manny intoned, "From the most mysterious regions of uncharted Asia, I give you the Chinese Cabinet of Metamorphosis!" The spotlight fell on Gypsy as she folded her huge wings and lowered herself into a Chinese food take-out box.

P. T. was excited. The show was back on track! "Rosie! The whole troupe, onstage for the finale!"

Rosie was bandaging Dim's hurt foot. "I just need a little time—"

"Now!" P. T. cried.

Dim and Rosie hurried to make their entrance. Rosie paused to speak to a pair of balls in a pile of props. "Tuck! Roll! We're up next!"

The balls popped open. Ta-da! The identical Hungarian pill bugs sprang to attention and rolled into a shoulder stand. The pill bugs didn't speak much English, but they loved to perform and argue.

Meanwhile, Manny summoned the voice of Confucius. The fly audience was not impressed. "Get off the stage, you old hack!" Manny's composure was shattered.

"I demand to know who said that!" the mantis thundered.

In reply, a chunk of ripe tomato splattered in Manny's face. The crowd laughed, then started booing.

"Ingrates!" Manny shouted as he left the arena.

Gypsy was still in the takeout box. "Manny?" her muffled voice called. When there was no answer, the moth wriggled the box offstage.

A fly in the audience complained, "I've only got twenty-four hours to live. I ain't gonna waste it here! C'mon!"

This started a general exit. P. T. panicked. "I've just about had it with these losers," he muttered, seizing a matchstick. P. T. hopped back on the thimble and screamed, "FLAM-ING DEATH!"

The flies stopped, curious.

P. T. continued, "I hold in my hand the match that decides whether two bugs live or die this very evening!"

The flies turned to watch. The ringmaster relished the attention. He had his crowd. "In a moment, I will light this trail of matches leading to a sheet of flypaper doused in lighter fluid."

Slim gestured to the flypaper. Heimlich and Francis jumped up and down on a small can of lighter fluid. The flammable liquid squirted onto the sticky sheet.

P. T. went on, "Aimed directly at the flypaper are Tuck and Roll, the pill bug cannon balls!"

"Ta-Daaa!" In the side ring, the pill bugs grinned and posed beside an eyedropper cannon.

Nearby, the giant Dim perched atop a roofing nail, poised to leap onto the dropper's rubber squeeze bulb. The rhino beetle waved to the audience.

"The cannon will be triggered by Dim, trained to jump at the sound of this bell, set to go off in fifteen seconds." P. T. pointed at an oven timer where Gypsy lounged. Manny twisted the timer's giant dial, which started ticking loudly.

The flies were fascinated as P. T. built to his climax. "Our pill bugs' only hope of survival is our Mistress of the High Wire, Rosie!"

The shy spider waved sheepishly at the crowd from her position atop the center pole.

"Secured to a web line of the exact length, Rosie will plummet down to these two posts." P. T. waved his arms at two pencils stuck in the ground like goalposts halfway between the cannon and the flypaper. "She will spin a web of safety in less than fifteen seconds. Not good enough, you say? Well, what if they were all"—P. T. paused for effect, then yelled—"blindfolded!"

The ringmaster struck the match with a *scritch* of sulfur. The bright flame sizzled as the performers pulled on blindfolds. The audience leaned on the edges of their seats.

Precision timing, daring feats, and possible disaster: this they had to see!

What P. T. Flea didn't see was Tuck and Roll having yet another squabble. The passionate pill bugs were already at the shoving stage, but P. T. hadn't noticed. The ringmaster rattled on. "Ladies and gentlebugs, may I suggest that those of you with weak constitutions leave the arena. This act is so dangerous that if the slightest thing should go wrong . . . "

Roll shoved Tuck off the platform where he bounced into P. T. The flea dropped his lit match and the trail of matches blazed.

P. T. gasped. "No!"

High on the center pole, the blindfolded Rosie thought she heard "GO!" The spider bungee-jumped to the pencils and started frantically spinning a web.

Tuck next collided with Manny, who fell against the timer. Gypsy yelped as she slid off the device. Trying to regain his balance, Manny's groping hands pushed the timer dial forward. DING!

As trained, Dim jumped at the bell's toll.

40

Roll was only halfway into the cannon when the rhino beetle landed on the dropper. POW! Roll hit P. T., who found himself hurtling toward the flypaper, just as Rosie said, "Done!"

She was done, but she wasn't finished. The blindfolded spider had no idea her web had a huge hole in the center.

The web failed to stop P. T. as he streaked through the air to land on the flypaper with a sticky THWACK! The roly-poly flea desperately tried to free himself as crackling orange flames lunged toward him. The flypaper crisped, curled, and turned black behind a wall of Flaming Death. "Get me out of here!" P. T. yelped.

The frightened clowns scrambled for water, but the buffoons only collided with each other. The audience roared with laughter. They thought the disaster was part of the act!

Just before the flames reached the sticky trap, P. T. pulled himself free. He laughed with relief—then the flypaper fell over!

The sticky sheet flopped onto the blazing

matches. FOOF! The audience gasped with delight at the fiery spectacle.

The paper burned in a quick flash, leaving P. T. scorched and frozen in surprise. The performers rushed to help their blackened boss.

Rosie quickly apologized, "It's the web. I'm sorry!"

Way too late, the clowns arrived bearing beads of water. "Here we come, P. T.!" They doused the charred flea from three different directions. SPLASH! SPLASH! SPLASH!

There was a spatter of polite applause from the stand. "Burn him again!" a fly urged.

The following morning, P. T. stood beside his cookie box wagon. "You're fired!" he shouted.

"Give us another chance," Francis pleaded.

P. T. had heard that too many times before. The fried flea just glared at his circus bugs. His voice was unnaturally calm. "You guys are a lost cause. You will never, ever be any good." P. T. climbed to the driver's seat and snapped a whip above his team of millipedes. "Hai-yah! Giddyap!"

Having no idea what their leader had just said, the Hungarian pill bugs waved good-bye with cheerful enthusiasm as P. T.'s wagon lurched away. The rest of the circus bugs were stunned. What would they do now?

Chapter 5

"Wow! The City!" Flik had never seen the City before. The buildings were big. The lights were bright. Yellow beetles scurried through the streets and throngs of bugs rushed everywhere.

Of course, to human eyes the City was nothing more than a pile of junk: old boxes, paint cans, and other cast-off clutter. But Flik saw an exciting metropolis where he was sure to find his fighters.

"Get out and stay out!" someone shouted.

Across the street, Flik saw a bug tossed out of a rough-looking joint made from a rusty paint can with bullet holes punched in the sides. Flik grinned. A place that shabby and mean was just the sort of hangout where an ant could find some tough customers.

And Flik was right. Inside the dimly lit dive, thirsty bugs tossed back Black Flags, straight up.

A tough louse chuckled. "Hair of the dog you bit."

Flik made a beeline for the bar, eager to complete his mission. He sidled up to a mosquito and asked if the scary-looking insect wanted to help the ant colony. But the whiny mosquito sucked up a Bloody Mary and passed out. Flik searched the room for other prospects.

Not far away, the newly fired circus bugs sat at a rusty table.

"P. T.'s right. We stink," Francis groaned.

Slim was just as depressed. "We weren't looking for much, just a little spotlight to call our own."

Heimlich shoved a whole leaf in his mouth. He talked around the green wad. "Someday I will be a beautiful butterfly. Then everything will be better."

Manny felt it was no use prolonging the inevitable. The bugs had been together for a long time, but the act was breaking up. Manny lifted his drink in a toast and said, "Farewell, my friends!"

Gypsy was choked up. "But we've always been together."

"We've always been bad," Francis said glumly.

"At least we were consistent." Rosie tried for cheer.

Before they could drink the toast, Slim noticed the two nasty flies who had heckled them at the show. They were partying with a giant horsefly. "Francis, your boyfriends are here," Slim muttered.

To the circus bugs' dismay, the hecklers came straight to their table. "Hello there, girly bug," one said.

Francis dismissed them. "Shoo, fly! Don't bother me."

The other said, "Say, why don't you tell our pal, Thud, what you said at the circus—something about buzzing around a dung heap?" The hecklers yanked Francis's wings, chanting "Ladybug, ladybug, fly away home."

"Not so tough now, are you?" the first fly taunted.

"All right, clown, get up and fight like a girl," his buddy said.

Francis muttered directions under his

breath. "Get ready for the Sherwood Forest bit."

"No more playing props!" Slim protested futilely.

But Francis had already grabbed the unwilling walking stick. The manly ladybug suddenly stood up, brandishing Slim like a sword. "Hazzah!" Francis cried. "Stand back! We're the greatest warriors in all the shire! Come, Little John!"

Heimlich grabbed a toothpick from an olive. "What ho, Robin!"

"Let us dispose of these ill-tempered maggots!" Francis was badly overacting, but the trick worked! Francis and Heimlich leaped heroically at the pesky flies. The flies were so surprised, they jumped back.

The rest of the customers scattered to make room for the fight. Betting bugs were already figuring the odds. Everyone jostled for a better view.

Flik was shoved toward the entrance. "No, wait! I want to watch this," the ant objected. Flik could hardly believe his good luck.

"Warrior bugs!" he exclaimed, even as he was pushed out the door.

Flik heard one of the heroes shout, "You have robbed from the poor for too long!"

Flik was impressed. But Thud, the huge horsefly, was not. He simply growled and advanced on his merry adversaries.

Slim fretted. "Me thinketh it's not working!"

Heimlich agreed. "Retreat to the forest!"

The circus bugs turned to run. They were performers, not fighters. When push came to shove, they would rather take a bow and make an exit. But the doorway was jammed with spectators.

The only escape was up the paint can wall! The circus bugs scrambled to the top of the dive, but they only succeeded in tipping over the entire place.

The can tumbled onto its side, barrelling like a freight train down the street. The circus bugs ran in place like hamsters in a wheel. Their pounding feet rolled the can faster and faster, and everyone else was tossed around like laundry in a drier.

Then the can smacked into something solid. BOOM! CLANG! The contents of the can crashed. The circus bugs landed on top of a heap of junk and moaning, groaning insects.

Flik staggered to his feet, dizzy and thrilled. He looked up just in time to see Francis pull Slim from the pile as a glorious shaft of light shone down on a heroic tableau of Victorious Warriors. These were heroes indeed!

"Wow!" Flik breathed. He hurried up to the circus bugs. "That was the most incredible performance!" he gushed.

"Don't be makin' fun of us, kid," Francis growled.

"I mean it!" Flik said. "You guys were unbelievable."

Heimlich basked in the praise. He crushed Flik in a bear hug. "You liked us! You really, really liked us!"

"You guys are perfect." Flik gasped for breath and the caterpillar released him. "I've been scouting all over for bugs with your talent!"

The circus bugs completely misunderstood

Flik's intentions. The performers assumed Flik was in showbiz, too.

Gypsy whispered, "A talent scout!"

"Go on, go on," Francis urged. The bugs had never gotten a good review before. Maybe this was their big break at last!

"I'm from an ant colony just east of here," Flik started. He began to explain that grasshoppers were coming to Ant Island at the end of the season. "We're really low on food, and we don't know what to do," he continued.

Slim noticed Thud rising from the rubble. "Why don't you explain it on the way there," the walking stick suggested. The rest of the circus bugs hustled the inventor ant outside, keeping a wary eye on the huge horsefly stumbling after them.

"Don't you want to hear the details?" Flik asked, as the bugs prepared to fly.

Thud lumbered within reach.

"Yes, we love details!" Slim agreed. He tossed Flik onto Dim's broad back beside Heimlich, Tuck, Roll, and Rosie the spider.

"Hold on, Mr. Ant," Dim rumbled. He

spread his wings and took off with a deafening HUMMMM! The backwash knocked Thud on his back. The bugs had escaped!

"This is too good to be true!" Flik exclaimed.

Of course, it was! During the flight, Flik thought he explained everything to his fellow passengers. But the loud drone of Dim's wings drowned out Flik's speech. The only two bugs who could actually hear him were the Hungarian pill bugs, who didn't understand a word Flik said. The ant believed he had his warriors, and the circus bugs were convinced they had a gig at a dinner theater in the country.

Chapter 6

"Forget it, Dot, that loser is never comin' back," a pesky ant boy teased the tiny princess. Dot pretended she didn't hear him and scanned the sky with Flik's telescope.

Under the late summer sun, the heat beat down on Ant Island. Exhausted workers struggled to find food that wasn't there. Despair hung in the air like a dark cloud and workers dropped in their tracks. Corny and Thorny argued and complained. They pointed out that leaves were already falling. "We need a miracle," they told Princess Atta. The colony would never have enough food for the grasshoppers, much less themselves.

Only Dot still dared to hope that the colony would survive. Then, in the shimmering drop of the telescope's lens, she spotted her hero. "He did it! Flik did it!" the little ant suddenly exclaimed. Dot ran to spread the good news.

The ants panicked. When Dim's shadow covered the hill, they thought the grasshoppers had returned! The frantic ants hurried to hide, so only Dot was left to greet Flik and his newfound friends. "I knew you could do it," the little princess declared.

The rest of the colony cautiously peeked at the new arrivals.

Mr. Soil could not believe his eyes. "Flik has returned with savage insects!"

Atta was shocked. "He wasn't supposed to actually *find* someone."

Ant children swarmed the strange visitors. They marveled at Gypsy's wings and were awestruck by the humongous Dim, who seemed a ferocious giant. Excitement spread through the colony.

Council members crowed. Flik had finally done something right—and just in time! Even the Queen was pleased.

But Princess Atta wasn't so sure. Ants never fought grasshoppers. That was so . . . unantly.

Atta didn't like the idea of strangers fighting for the colony.

The circus bugs took the council's whispered debate as a sign that they might lose the job. Francis hastily mounted Dim's horn and announced, "Your Majesty, ladies and gentlebugs, pupae and larvae of all ages, our troupe guarantees a performance like no other. Why, when your grasshopper friends get here, we're going to knock them dead!"

At that, the colony cheered! The circus bugs basked in a wave of thunderous applause.

That very afternoon, the ants celebrated with a lavish banquet. The circus bugs enjoyed the privilege of sitting at the royal table with the Queen and Atta. Flik was thrilled to be seated beside the pretty princess.

Atta was still not convinced that any of this would work. But everyone was having a great time.

Then Mr. Soil's second-grade class presented the alleged warriors with a leaf mural of a bloody battle between bugs and grasshoppers.

"We drew one of you dying because our

teacher said it would be more dramatic," a little ant explained to the confused performers.

Then the gory mural was pulled aside to reveal schoolbugs dressed in homemade costumes. As Mr. Soil played the lute, the tiny ants enacted the coming war. By the end of the bloody pageant, all of the players lay "dead" on the stage.

The crowd loved the gruesome spectacle. They acted as if their enemies were already dead. The ants were ecstatic, but the circus bugs were in shock. What was going on?

Then Princess Atta made a speech. Her voice was too soft and no one could hear her. Ever helpful, Flik improvised a megaphone out of a leaf and some twigs.

Atta fumbled with the unfamiliar device. When she regained her composure, Atta thanked the warriors for their help in the fight against the grasshoppers. Then she thanked Flik for his forthright thinking.

At that point, Flik took the megaphone and proceeded to make grand promises and bold brags. As Atta's and Flik's words sank in, it dawned on the circus bugs that the ants were serious—they really believed Dim, Rosie, and the others were there to fight grasshoppers!

Rosie desperately tried to get Flik's attention. "We're circus bugs!" she whispered in the inventor's antennae.

Flik turned away from the megaphone. "There's no circus around here," he told the spider.

Flik turned to resume his speech to the colony, then Rosie's words sank in. Flik stalled. He shook Atta's hand. "Your Highness, the warriors have called for a secret meeting to plan for circus . . . um, circumventing the oncoming horde, so they can trapeze, uh, trap them with ease!"

"Shouldn't I come, too?" Atta asked.

"No!" Flik cried. "Heh, heh, it's classified in the DMZ. Gotta go ASAP, you know, strictly BYOB. Bye!"

The circus bugs rose to leave. A confused murmur spread through the colony. Atta did not look happy.

The flustered Flik gathered the circus bugs.

56

"If you'll all just follow me, please, right this way. I have to go now." He waved to the crowd. "Thanks again!"

Flik and the circus bugs beat a hasty exit into a stand of dried grass. Once safely out of earshot among the giant stalks, Flik screeched, "How can you be circus bugs?"

"Countless hours of practice, my boy," Manny said haughtily.

"I thought you were warriors!" Flik sputtered.

"What in the world would make you think that?" Rosie asked.

"You were running around that dive, screaming 'Hai-yah,' and knocking over customers like they were flies!" Flik explained.

"They *were* flies," Francis observed.

"You said you were going to knock grasshoppers dead," Flik added. "This, my friends, is false advertising!"

Manny was offended. "How dare you! You, sir, claimed to be a talent scout, preying upon the hungry souls of hapless *artistes*! Good day to you, sir!"

The troupe turned to leave, but not before Tuck and Roll angrily slapped Flik. The amazed ant tried to stop the bugs. "You can't go! You've got to help me! I'll think of something!"

Flik begged. He tried to explain all that was at stake. The colony would be destroyed. Flik would be branded with this mistake for the rest of his life. His children's children would be scorned by the whole colony. But Flik's pleas fell on deaf ears. The circus bugs didn't care.

Finally, Flik said, "Okay, but do me a favor before you leave. Just squish me! When they find out the truth, I'm as good as dead."

To make matters worse, Atta arrived. "I would like to speak with the so-called warriors."

"You can't! They're in the middle of a top-secret meeting, and they should not be disturbed. Right, guys?" Flik fibbed. He turned to see the last of the circus bugs disappearing between rustling blades of grass.

"Please don't go!" Flik cried, and he ran after the retreating bugs.

"I'm not going anywhere," Atta said. She was getting more suspicious by the minute.

Chapter 7

Dot perched atop a puffy dandelion. Through her tiny telescope, the little princess saw the circus bugs at the far bank of Ant Island. As the bugs spread wings and took flight, Flik jumped and grabbed the leg of the long, skinny bug.

Dot didn't know what was going on. Was this some secret warrior practice? Dot wanted to find out!

The princess plucked a piece of fluff and held it to the wind the way Flik had. With the first breeze, Dot was sailing to join her hero.

Flik knew the strangers were flying directly into danger. But as usual, no one would listen to him. Just as the inventive ant had feared, the bugs were heading straight for the hungry sparrow who lived across the river from Ant Island.

The circus bugs saw the sparrow just as it shrieked an antenna-splitting SCREECH. Manny groaned. "Oh, goody! Just when everything was going our way."

With a flap of its giant wings, the feathered monster took to the air. The bugs scurried along the riverbed, seeking shelter from the sharp beak stabbing at them like lightning from a dark, feathered cloud.

Still clinging to her fluff, Princess Dot wafted into the midst of the chaos. All the way over, the eager youngster had practiced flapping her tiny wings. Flight was even more glorious than she had hoped!

Dot looked down between her dangling feet to better savor the sensation of height. She saw Flik and the warriors leaving a cloud of dust as they beat feet for Ant Island. Now what were they doing? She would have to change direction to catch up with her hero.

Dot looked up just as the sparrow swooped down at her with an open beak. The princess let go of the dandelion seed just before the terrible jaws snapped shut.

Dot dropped like a stone, certain to be squished if someone did not save her. Strong arms suddenly seized her, and she heard a loud OOF!

Francis the ladybug caught Dot inches above the hard-packed soil. On impact, the bug skidded backward and tumbled into a gorge. Sand and pebbles rolled over the edge. Francis landed with a *thud* and a heavy pebble pinned his leg. Another tumbled on top of his head. Francis was down for the count.

"Miss ladybug, please wake up!" Dot slapped Francis's face. When he didn't respond, she remembered her Blueberry Scout training. While the bird's beak pecked all around her, the brave little princess freed Francis's leg and dragged him to safety.

Suddenly the sparrow was distracted by Heimlich and Slim. Together, the clowns pretended to be a fat, juicy worm on a stick.

"Yoo-hoo!" Heimlich called. Slim strained at his burden. "I'm going to snap. I just know it!"

With the bird's attention focused on the

tasty bait, Flik led the rest of the bugs in a heroic rescue. Hanging underneath Dim, Rosie used her webbing to lower Flik, Tuck, and Roll into the gorge.

The three insects lifted Francis and Dot into a spiderweb net. Then Dim soared away, with Francis, Dot, Flik, Tuck, and Roll dangling beneath him.

But the danger wasn't over for everyone. Slim and Heimlich were supposed to tease the bird, then get out of the way. Unfortunately, Slim's hiding place was too narrow for the chubby caterpillar.

"Help! Help! I'm too hungry to be eaten!" Heimlich moaned.

The sparrow swooped down for the kill, but was scared off by the frightening face adorning Gypsy's spread wings. The moth flew off just as Heimlich sucked in his gut far enough to fit through the crack.

In the air, Dim buzzed straight into a dry, thorny bush. The sparrow stopped short, fearing the prickly branches, and the bugs were safe at last.

"What's that sound?" Rosie asked. She didn't hear the rustling of leaves or the patter of rain. This was a nice sound.

"That, my friends, is the sound of applause," Manny explained.

The circus bugs had never heard such sweet music! They leaned over the branch where they had found shelter and saw a horde of cheering ants.

Atta and the Council Members had seen the whole fight. The heroic deeds of these great warriors inspired the colony to applause.

The love of an audience roused Francis from his stupor. "Am I in heaven?" the manly ladybug wondered.

The bugs who had endured so much abuse at the feet of dull flies were overwhelmed with the exuberant adoration.

"Our Blueberry Troop salutes you bugs. And to Miss Francis, we honor you by adding spots to our bandanas. We voted you honorary den mother," a squeaky voice shrilled.

Francis was a little confused. He knew

Princess Dot's troop meant well, but the manly bug didn't think he'd make a very good mother. Still, all the little shining eyes and the flowers crowding his sickroom were enchanting enough to make a bug choke up.

Dr. Flora broke in, ushering the Blueberries out of the patient's room. "All right, girls. He needs his rest."

Francis lay in the ant clinic with his broken leg suspended in a leaf cast. The heroic ladybug was surrounded by all his circus friends, Flik, and Princess Atta. The ladybug was happy. He had performed before royalty!

Atta took Flik aside to apologize for doubting him. "When you first brought them here, I thought you'd hired a bunch of clowns," the princess confessed. She simply wanted to avoid another royal blunder. "Sometimes it's like the whole colony is watching me, waiting for me to . . ."

"Mess up?" Flik prompted.

The princess suddenly understood how Flik always felt. "How would you like to be the warrior bugs' personal assistant?" Atta offered. "You have a great rapport with them. That rescue was very brave."

Flik was a little embarrassed by all this praise. Praise was as foreign to him as applause was to the circus bugs.

"Not every bug would face a bird," Atta said gravely. "Even Hopper's afraid of them."

As Flik sputtered a modest denial, the idea of circus performers and birds came together with a bright flash of inspiration. "Say that again?" the inventor asked.

"Even Hopper's afraid of birds," Atta repeated dutifully.

Flik had a funny look on his face as he turned and ran. The princess was perplexed, and worried. That look meant Flik had an idea, and his ideas were dangerous!

Flik had a dangerous idea, all right, a wild idea, an idea only he could have, but he had to sell the circus bugs on it. If the colony knew the idea was Flik's, they would reject it automatically.

The circus bugs were a little resistant, but once they signed a few autographs, they decided that being warriors wasn't so bad after all. So "Major Manny" presented the plan to Atta and the Ant Council.

Atta in turn presented it to the colony, to overwhelming approval. Soon the ants were hard at work building Flik's idea—a bird!

The next step in "Major Manny's Plan" was to hoist the bird high above the anthill. When Hopper's gang appeared, they would deploy the decoy to frighten off the grasshoppers! No one would get hurt and the colony would be safe forever. All the ants had to do was what ants do best: WORK!

With nutshells, acorns, sap, leaves, long sticks and short, the colony constructed the framework for a hollow bird. The circus bugs, who were used to working together, adapted easily to colony life. Their unique talents contributed to the building of the bird. Rosie's spider silk secured the frame.

The circus bugs also helped contruct a launch platform in the knothole of the tree that towered above the anthill. Dim used his wings as a leafblower to clear out the dark hollow. Flik had designed the complicated contraption to send the fake bird soaring at the key moment. Once the framework was complete, the ants used leaves to mimic feathers. Before long, Flik's bird was being raised to the knothole launcher.

All of their hard work had paid off. The job was done! The ants celebrated with a jubilant party.

A few dedicated workers remained vigilant. Thorny was among the sentries scanning the horizon with Flik's rolled-leaf telescopes.

Meanwhile, the idle grasshoppers lazed at a sunny resort far away. The gang had food, sunshine, and bugs to push around. Some of them urged Molt to ask Hopper why they should bother returning to Ant Island. Wasn't their tropical paradise enough?

"There was an ant there that stood up to me," Hopper said.

Loco laughed. "Just one puny ant."

"If you let one puny ant stand up to you,

then they'll all stand up," Hopper stated. A light blazed in his good eye. "Those puny ants outnumber us a hundred to one. If they ever figure that out, there goes our way of life. It's not about food. It's about keeping the ants in line. That's why we're going back! Let's ride!"

The ant party was just winding down when Flik approached the circus bugs. Now that the bird was built, he had a plan that would let the performing bugs sneak out unseen. They could leave without further risk.

"Dim don't want to go," the big beetle rumbled.

Rosie reasoned that she would need to stay in the ant colony to take care of Dim. And Francis had kind of promised the Blueberries that he'd teach them more card games—and make them stop beating up the boys.

"It would seem we've been booked for an extended engagement," said Gypsy.

In short, the circus bugs didn't want to leave. Even Tuck and Roll felt at home. Ta-daaa!

Princess Atta was pleased. "Will you look at this colony? I don't even recognize them. And I have you bugs to thank for it. Actually, I have to thank you, Flik."

Flik was surprised by Atta's sudden appearance and kind words. His antennae got tangled with Atta's. The two ants blushed and pulled away from each other awkwardly. It was obvious to every bug that the two had feelings for each other.

BA-WOOOO! BA-WOOOO!

The party stopped. Everyone's antennae perked up. The snail shell alarm meant danger!

Thorny had seen luminous mushroom signals from more remote sentries. His telescope revealed bright lights approaching the anthill.

Princess Atta shouted. "Battle stations, everyone! This is not a drill!"

Every ant knew its job. They scrambled, ready for action.

But the ants did not expect what arrived through the root gateway.

"Whoooa! Whooa! Steady, girl!"

The circus bugs froze where they stood. They knew that voice. They cried in chorus, "Oh, no! It's P. T.!"

True enough, there atop his brightly colored cookie box wagon, was their old boss. The cricket band played and the lightning bug spotlights glowed. P. T. waved his top hat and declared in his best ringmaster voice, "Greetings and salutations! I am the great P. T. Flea. I am in need of your assistance." The fat flea was tired. He sighed. "Oh, let's just cut to the chase."

The band stopped and the lights went out. P. T. said, "Look, you're the twenty-seventh ant colony I've seen this week. I'm looking for a bunch of circus performers. Have you seen 'em?"

"No!" Flik yelled. "I'm sorry, no. No one's ever seen anyone like that around here. I guess you have a lot more anthills to check. Bye."

The flea unrolled a colorful poster. "Are you sure? They look something like this."

"Wait a second. Ain't that Staff Sergeant Slim?" Corny asked.

While Flik tried to cover up the poster, the circus bugs slid under a leaf. The leaf inched past the cookie box wagon toward the root gateway.

But there was no fooling an old showbug like the flea. He lifted the leaf and cried, "Guys! I've been lookin' all over for you. Flaming Death is a huge hit! Word got around. The next day there was a line of flies outside the tent that went on forever. Must've been a foot long."

Despite the bugs' best efforts to shush him, P. T.'s loud enthusiasm carried to the colony. "We'll be the top circus act in the business!"

P. T.'s words hung in the silence like a circus billboard. At last Atta spoke. "You're not warriors?"

"Are you kiddin'?" P. T. laughed. "These guys are the lousiest circus bugs you've ever seen. And they're gonna make me rich!"

Thorny almost choked on his words. "Our entire defense strategy was concocted by clowns?"

"Hey!" Francis said sternly. "Flik's idea could work!"

The silence that followed was even more ominous. The ladybug had really put a foot in his proboscis.

Mr. Soil panicked. "The last leaf is about to fall!"

"We haven't collected any food for Hopper," Dr. Flora added.

"We'll have to dip into our emergency reserve," Corny gasped.

Atta didn't listen to any of the distraught council members. She was bewildered by the turn of events.

Thorny fretted. "If Hopper finds out . . . "

But the Queen stepped forward. "Hopper is not going to find out," she declared. "We will hide all this and pretend it never happened. You bugs were never here, so I suggest you leave."

"The bird will work," Flik insisted.

"I never thought I'd see the day when an ant would put himself before the rest of his colony," the Queen said sadly.

"I just wanted to get the bird built," Flik explained.

"You lied to us," the Queen stated.

"But only about the bugs. Not about the bird!"

Atta lost her patience with Flik. She had given him one chance too many. "You lied to the Queen. You lied to the colony. You lied to me. And like an idiot I believed you."

"I was afraid you'd think I was a loser," Flik said helplessly.

"I want you to leave," Atta said firmly. "And this time, don't come back."

"Tough crowd," P. T. muttered. He cracked his whip and the circus wagon lurched forward. "Giddyap!" The circus bugs trudged in the dust behind the gaudy wagon. Flik trailed after the performers.

The hatred of the colony was concentrated on Flik, like sunlight focused to deadly fury by a magnifying glass. Only Princess Dot shed a tear.

As the wagon rumbled away, the last leaf fell.

Chapter 8

"Hopper won't accept this!" Atta was horrified. Throughout the foggy morning, worker ants had labored, dragging grain to the offering stone once again. But the pile was much too small. Thorny told her that was all they could spare or the colony would starve that winter.

Then the ants heard a dull drone in the sky. Their doom had arrived. The buzzing grew louder, then suddenly stopped. One by one, the huge grasshoppers appeared like evil spirits out of the fog.

Hopper stalked to the offering stone. He held the meager pile of grain over his head and bellowed, "You little termites! I gave you a second chance and this is all I get?" Hopper tossed the grain at the colony. "Have you been playing all summer? You think this is a game?"

The grasshopper gang charged through the ant tunnels and burst the barricade that protected the storerooms.

"This wasn't part of the deal!" Atta protested. "We'll starve!"

Hopper shoved the princess into the food piles. "Pick up my food now!" he commanded.

The Queen would have helped her daughter, but Hopper took the elderly bug by her arm. "You stay with me, Your Highness."

Hopper had plans. Every ant in the colony was put to work. Hopper vowed no one would sleep until he got every scrap of food on Ant Island.

But not every ant had been at the party. Princess Dot and the Blueberries huddled in their secret clubhouse, hidden in a clump of grass. The little ants held their breath as two grasshopper goons searched the area for any escapees.

Dot overheard the grasshoppers' plans. "We'll be out of here before it rains," she heard one big bug say.

"The plan is, we work them till they drop.

Then we squish the queen to remind them who's boss!" the other concluded smugly.

"Oh, cool!"

Dot waited until the goons were gone. "I'm gonna get help," she told her friends before slipping out the clubhouse's secret passage.

Almost immediately, Dot encountered the monstrous Thumper. The brave Blueberry defended herself and escaped. But then the grasshopper herded her toward the very cliff where Flik had first left Ant Island.

Dot was trapped between vicious grasshoppers and empty air! She jerked her wings in a desperate attempt to fly, but her feet barely left the ground.

Thumper cackled behind Dot. She felt hot breath on the back of her neck. Dot had no choice. She jumped off the cliff!

Thumper laughed and laughed, then flew away.

The setting sun glowed on the bright colors of the circus wagon lurching over the landscape. A very happy P. T. Flea sang as he drove the wagon. The circus owner's mood was not shared by his ant passenger. Flik felt low as an earthworm's tummy.

The clowns tried to cheer him up, but the lonely ant was inconsolable.

Then a familiar voice cried, "Flik!"

The downcast ant looked up and saw Dot buzzing through the air. The little princess was flying!

Out of breath, she dropped onto the wagon and panted, "You have to come back! Hopper moved into the anthill. The gang is eating everything!"

"Good heavens!" Manny exclaimed in horror.

"And I heard them say that when they're finished, Hopper's gonna squish my mom!" Dot concluded.

"How dreadful!" the mantis gasped.

"What should we do?" Francis asked.

"The bird!" Gypsy cried.

"The bird won't work," Flik muttered miserably. He slumped in a dark corner of the wagon. Nothing he built ever worked.

"What're you talking about?" Francis demanded. "It was your idea."

Dot began, "You said everything—"

"Forget everything I ever told you," Flik said bitterly. "Let's face it. The colony was right. I just make things worse. That bird is a guaranteed failure, just like me."

Manny was indignant. "My boy, I have made a living out of being a failure. And you, sir, are not a failure."

"You've done so many good things," Rosie asserted.

"Show me one thing I've done right," Flik challenged.

There was a small, awful silence, broken only by Dim's dim "Uh . . ."

"Dim is right, my boy," Manny said cheerfully. "You have rekindled the long-dormant embers of purpose in our lives."

"If not for you," Slim said, "Francis would never have gotten in touch with his feminine side."

"Oh, yeah?" Francis growled. But he considered for a moment, fondly recalling his times with the Blueberry Troop. Francis said, "You know what? He's right."

Gypsy made a perfect military salute. "Lieutenant Gypsy reporting for duty."

"Kid, say the word and we'll follow you into battle," Francis added.

"We believe in you, my boy," Manny declared.

But not even Dot's pleas would change Flik's mind. Flik looked up only when she brought him a pebble.

"Pretend it's a seed," Dot said, recalling their long-ago conversation in the field. The little rock made the difference. Flik stood up. "Let's do it!" he said.

"What's with the rock?" Francis asked Slim.

The walking stick shrugged. "Must be an ant thing."

Flik exclaimed, "First, let's turn this box of cookies around!"

Chapter 9

"They haven't discovered the bird," Flik whispered. He was observing the ant colony through a grass telescope. Flik was pleased. The Queen was alive but most of the colony had been forced into slave labor.

The grasshoppers feasted on their stolen food. The big bugs were completely confident in their conquest of Ant Island.

Turning the wagon around had been a simple matter. Right now, P. T. was trussed in the wagon, slung from the ceiling, begging, "Guys! Get me out of this thing. I promise to start paying you."

On the return trip, Flik had briefed his bug buddies. As soon as Flik and Dot rounded up the Blueberries, it was time to set the plan in motion.

* * *

The grasshoppers were munching away when they heard a dramatic drumroll beyond the darkened root gateway.

"Ladies and gentlemen, larvae of all stages . . . " a voice intoned. "Rub your legs together for the world's greatest bug circus!"

The band blared a jaunty tune as the circus parade marched out of the darkness and right up to Hopper's table.

Hopper stood up. "Wait a minute! What's going on around here?"

Frightened, Atta didn't know what to say, but Slim spoke up. "We were invited by Princess Atta as a surprise for your arrival."

"You've got to be kidding," Hopper said suspiciously.

A nervous Dim bumped into the eyedropper cannon and Tuck and Roll were launched through the air. The pill bugs bounced off the side of the circus wagon. They turned perfect somersaults and landed in front of Hopper with a cheerful "Hey! Ta-daaa!"

They danced for the big bug. When the pill

bugs noticed the audience was sitting in stony silence, they blamed each other and fell to fighting.

Hopper enjoyed that. "It's funny when the little bugs hit each other." He chuckled. "I guess we could use a little entertainment. Looks like you did something right for once, Princess."

"On with the show!" Slim cried. And the band resumed playing.

First up was Dim with Tuck and Roll. The riding act and the clowns' slapstick got the grasshoppers laughing. No one noticed Flik and the Blueberries climbing up to the bird launchpad.

As Manny's magic act began, Flik settled into the bird's cockpit. The Blueberries sat on benches in the bird's body. They rested their tiny hands on the oars that would flap the wings.

Flik ran through a final checklist as, far below, Manny announced, "From the most mysterious regions of uncharted Asia, I give you the Chinese Cabinet of Metamorphosis!"

Manny covered his eyes with one hand and stalked among the banquet tables. "Utilizing psychic vibrations, I shall select the perfect volunteer."

"Ooh! Ooh! Pick me!" Molt begged.

But Manny walked past the molting grasshopper, as if in a trance. Manny's extended palm pointed to the Queen. "Why, Your Majesty!" the magician said in perfect surprise.

Thumper growled when the mantis took the Queen's hand. But Hopper shushed the savage bug. "Let her go. Maybe he'll saw her in half."

Manny escorted the Queen to his Chinese take-out box. The magician helped the elderly insect climb Dim's horn. Manny said, "As you ascend the dung beetle to the unknown, put your trust in the mysteries that are beyond mere mortal comprehension."

Dim lifted his horn and the Queen was raised to the top of the box. Then she vanished inside the white cardboard carton.

"Oh, this is gonna be good!" Hopper laughed.

"I call upon the ancient Szechuan spirits to inhabit the body of our volunteer," Manny chanted. He raised his hands above his head. Storm clouds began to cover the moon. Thunder rumbled as the magician cried, "Transformation!"

"Wow! Manny's gettin' good," Francis remarked as the mantis finished with a dramatic flourish.

"And now, Insectus Transformatus!" The box shook. Then the top popped and Gypsy fluttered out. The frightening face on her fluttering wings astounded the grasshoppers.

As Gypsy took her bows, she opened and shut her wings repeatedly. That was the signal Flik was waiting for. The Queen was safely hidden under Dim's carapace. Time to launch the bird.

Flik's launch mechanism used a rock to flip a lever that would fling the bird into the air. At the crucial moment, though, the stone got stuck.

That small delay was just enough time for Hopper to get suspicious. "Where's the Queen?" he asked.

"I'm sorry. A magician never reveals his secrets," Manny coolly replied to his frightening audience.

"That's very true, boss," Molt agreed. "I mean, where would the mystery be if we all knew how . . . "

A single glance from Hopper was enough to silence his brother. "I said, where is she?" Hopper repeated as he choked Manny.

At that moment, two ant boys were frantically trying to free the bird launch mechanism. Then, with a sudden *SNAP* and a *POP*, everything fell into place, and the fake bird flew! Flik and the Blueberries screamed as their craft plunged straight down.

The Blueberries pumped at the wing oars. Amplified by snail shells, the troop's scream sounded like the screech of an attacking bird of prey.

Hopper looked up to see his worst nightmare hurtling straight toward him—a hungry bird! The grasshoppers scattered like roaches at the flick of a kitchen light.

Flik and the Blueberries had regained

control of the bird. They turned to make another pass. Hopper cowered behind his scaly brother. The circus bugs performed their well-rehearsed terror, complete with fake blood and horrifying screams.

Some of the brighter ants realized what was going on. They joined in the theatrics by squishing red juicy berries onto their bodies and screaming in dramatic anguish.

Hopper ran like the coward he was. But everywhere he turned, the terrified bully saw horribly mutilated bugs. All Hopper could hear was the rush of wings in the air and the awful screech of that creature.

In the excitement, no one noticed that P. T. had managed to wriggle out of Rosie's web. The circus owner looked out a wagon window and saw Manny "dying" in Gypsy's arms.

"There goes my magic act!" P. T. fretted. Then he screamed in terror when he saw the bird zoom by. His whole circus could be swallowed up in seconds. The antsy flea leaped from the wagon just as the bird smashed the cookie box.

The tough old showbug had visited twenty-seven anthills to find his act and he wasn't about to let some starling eat his stars. Circus props were strewn all over the ground. P. T. seized a match, scraped it against a stone, and as the sulfur flared, he cried, "FLAMING DEATH!"

The flea sprang into the air. He landed heavily on the can of lighter fluid and the combustible concoction squirted from the nozzle. Touched with the match, the stream turned into a river of flame. Flik's bird caught fire!

Flik and the Blueberries were forced to abandon the mission and the bird crashed to the ground. Poor Flik! Another scheme had gone down in flames.

Blueberries swarmed from the wreckage of the colony's last hope.

"Nice goin', P. T.," Francis grumbled.

"How was I supposed to know?" asked the astonished flea.

As Dot crawled from the flaming ruins, Hopper's powerful hands grabbed her. Hopper waved the little princess so all could see. "Did you think you could get away with this?" he bellowed.

"I'm the one you want," Flik said. "The bird was all my idea."

Hopper tossed Dot aside and cut Thumper's leash. Like a rabid pit bull, the mad grasshopper charged Flik. The ant was malled, thrashed, and chewed like a piece of rawhide.

Hopper raved, "Where did you get the gall to do this to me?"

Flik managed to rise. "You were gonna squish the Queen."

"I hate when someone gives away the ending," Hopper sneered. Thumper resumed beating the brave ant.

Hopper snapped his fingers and the beating stopped. "You're lower than dirt," Hopper said. "You're an ant. And let this be a lesson to all you ants. Ideas are dangerous things. You were not meant to have ideas. You are mindless, soil-sucking losers, put on this earth to serve us. And we need to make sure you don't forget this. If I ever find . . . "

Hopper noticed the ants weren't listening to his speech. He turned and saw Flik wobbling to his feet. "You're wrong, Hopper. Somehow, year after year these ants manage to pick food for themselves *and* for you. Who's the weaker species? Ants weren't meant to serve grasshoppers. You need us, we don't need you! We're stronger than you say we are, and you know it."

Hopper was at a loss for words. With an angry scream, he attacked Flik.

In mere seconds, the grasshopper stood over his fallen foe. The great green grasshopper lifted his armored foot, ready to squish Flik.

Atta flew up to stand over the inventor. Hopper laughed at her foolish defiance.

"Uh, boss, I hate to interrupt," Molt said urgently.

His triumph spoiled, Hopper spun on his brother. Only then did the leader see that he was surrounded by the entire ant colony. Thousands of tiny heads and waving antennae, thousands of shiny carapaces and tough little arms hardened by years of work, thousands of hearts with one idea: Save the Queen!

"Get back!" Hopper shrieked.

Princess Atta was utterly calm and completely regal. "You see, Hopper," she told him, "nature has a certain order. The ants pick the food, the ants keep the food, and the grasshoppers . . . leave!"

Hopper had a point when he said that one ant was puny, and a hundred were not. The grasshoppers learned the truth of that as they were overwhelmed by the angry swarm of ants.

The circus bugs got in on the act, and even the Blueberries whipped their weight in grasshoppers.

Hopper knew he was defeated, but he would not surrender. Instead, he set his sights on capturing the Queen, but Rosie threw a silk lasso around the would-be Queen-napper. Hopper was quickly wrapped in a tight web and loaded into the cannon.

Suddenly, a giant drop of water smashed onto the soil.

"Rain!" Flik cried.

"Everyone to the anthill!" Atta commanded, as more drops fell like bombs.

For the next few moments, the fight was forgotten as everyone, Blueberries, circus bugs, and the whole colony, got safely underground. Dim was heading for safety when a raindrop knocked him into the cannon, launching Hopper into the air.

The grasshopper made a grab for Flik and flew him up into the tree. The circus bugs tried to rescue Flik, but the branches held them back. Hopper was getting away!

Just then, a blurry form flew past. Grabbing Flik, Atta dodged raindrops, but Hopper was still in pursuit.

Then Flik had another idea. After they landed on the riverbank, Flik hid the princess behind a leaf. "No matter what happens, stay down," he said. The ants were in the wild part of the island.

The inventor ran to meet the scowling Hopper. The grasshopper was dripping wet and still covered with cobwebs.

Flik trembled and quavered. "H-h-hopper. No, no, I didn't mean it. I'm so sorry, Hopper. Please don't!" The ant cowered, backing away into a tangle of twigs and grass. Flik begged for mercy, knowing that Hopper had none. But Hopper didn't know what Flik knew.

Skreee!!!!!

"What's this? Another one of your little bird tricks?" Hopper mocked as the clever ant shrank in fake cowardice against the wall of twigs. The hungry sparrow lived here.

"No, it's real," Flik assured his enemy. His plan was working.

Hopper looked up and realized the tangle of twigs was a nest. The last thing he saw was a huge bird beak closing around him.

Chapter 10

"Let's go! We've got a schedule to keep." P. T. Flea was getting his show on the road. He'd signed up a new ant acrobat team, and he had a new strongman: Hopper's brother, Molt.

The flaky grasshopper was grateful. "Thank you for the chance, Mr. Flea. You won't regret it. I've always wanted to be in showbiz."

"If you're going to be a strongman, make with the strong already," P. T. griped.

Molt carried the eyedropper cannon into the wagon and P. T. shut the door behind him. The circus owner spoke to Flik. "Sure I can't convince you to come along?"

"My place is here," Flik said confidently.

"Your loss," P. T. said, and he turned his attention to his crew.

P. T.'s usual performers hastened to load props into the newly repaired wagon.

"I'm not gonna cry. I'm not gonna cry," Francis repeated, as the Blueberries bid him good-bye. The manly ladybug was struggling with his tender feelings.

Flik thought Atta looked fine in the Queen's crown, although the she wasn't so sure. "Do I look official enough?" she worried.

"Let me adjust your crown a bit," Flik said.

And then Atta addressed the circus bugs. "Thanks to you all for giving us back our hope, our dignity, and our lives."

Slim was spokesperson for the circus. "And to you, Queen Atta, you have given us so much. Please accept this gift from us bugs to you ants." He proudly presented the royal ant with a rock.

"Well . . . it's a rock," Atta stammered.

The circus bugs beamed, certain that they had given the perfect gift.

Flik whispered to the puzzled queen, "I'll explain later." Then he turned to the circus bugs. "You'll never know how much you all mean."

P. T. was getting antsy. "Now it's getting

mushy. All right, everyone! There's paying customers out there."

P. T. cracked his whip. "Hai-ya!" The millipedes grunted and strained, then with a bump the wagon started to roll. Giant Dim's humming wings lifted him into the air.

"Oh, my gosh! We forgot Heimlich!" Slim exclaimed.

Even as the walking stick worried, the chubby caterpillar popped out of a cocoon. "I'm finished. Finally I am a beautiful butterfly," Heimlich declared.

If the truth be told, however, the caterpillar's change was far from miraculous. Tiny wings struggled to support his flabby bulk.

"The wagon's leaving!" Flik yelled to Heimlich. "You better start flying."

"I am flying," Heimlich asserted. "And from way up here, you all look like ants."

As the circus wagon rolled away through the fields, happy ant workers raised their new Flik harvesters in a twenty-one-grain salute.

The unique ant had been laughed at, ignored, banished, and beaten. But in the end,

Flik had triumphed! The colony was back—and better than before. Because one ant can make a difference, just as one little seed can sprout a mighty oak.